MARY-KATE & ASHLEY

Starring in

Billboard DAD

Novelization by Megan Stine

Based on the teleplay by
Maria Jacquemetton

A PARACHUTE PRESS BOOK

PARACHUTE
PRESS

Parachute Publishing, L.L.C
156 Fifth Avenue
Suite 302
New York, NY 10010

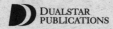
DUALSTAR
PUBLICATIONS

Dualstar Publications
c/o Thorne and Company
A Professional Law Corporation
1801 Century Park East, Twelfth Floor
Los Angeles, CA 90067

Troll Communications L.L.C.
100 Corporate Drive
Mahwah, NJ 07430

Book created and produced by Parachute Publishing, L.L.C.,
in cooperation with Dualstar Publications, a division of
Dualstar Entertainment Group, Inc.

ISBN 1-57351-006-8

First Printing: December 1999
Printed in the United States of America

10 9 8 7 6 5 4 3 2 1

CHAPTER ONE

It hit me one day at the beach. Right after I caught the most amazing wave and rode my surfboard all the way onto the sand.

"Hey, Emily!" a guy named Vinnie called after me. Vinnie was one of the surf hounds who hung around the beach. "Say hi to your dad for me, will you? I haven't seen him in like, forever."

"Sure, Vinnie," I called back. "I'll tell him."

If I can get Dad's attention, I thought.

That's when it hit me. It wasn't just Vinnie. *No one* had seen my dad in ages. Ever since my mom died two years ago, he almost never left the house. All he did was mope around his art studio.

My dad is Max Tyler, the famous sculptor.

I should back up a little. I'm Emily Tyler, and I have to admit I'm a pretty lucky kid. My twin sister Tess and I live in the greatest place you can imagine—Venice, California.

We've got the ocean right outside our door, and the famous Venice boardwalk. Tourists come here from all over the world, just to hang out. It's pretty awesome.

Our house is totally cool, too. My dad built it. We have super-high ceilings and a metal staircase leading up to our bedroom. Dad's studio is downstairs. Outside there's a courtyard with a fence around it. Dad used to work on his sculptures out there sometimes. But lately he'd been so gloomy, he didn't even do *that* anymore.

Not that Tess and I don't miss our mom a lot. Of course we do. But it was different for Dad, somehow. It seemed as if the longer she was gone, the sadder he got. And seeing Dad sad made *me* sad.

Right then and there, I decided it was time for all of that to change.

I grabbed my surfboard and Rollerblades and carried them to the boardwalk. Then I slipped on my skates and headed home. Tess and I had to make a plan. Our dad needed to get a life—and fast.

"Hey, Tess!" a voice called after me.

I spun around and saw Cody skating toward me. Cody lives three doors away from us. He has almost-black hair and eyes, and a nice smile.

He skated past me, slapping me a high five.

"I'm Emily," I corrected him.

"Oops," Cody said, a little embarrassed.

I don't know why Cody gets us confused. Sure, we're twins, but Tess and I are totally different. For one thing, Tess is better at most sports—except surfing. She's left-handed, I'm right-handed. She likes boys, I like boys.

Well, okay—so we have *some* things in common!

And there's one more thing we both agree about: We have the greatest dad in the world. That's why it was time to help him get a life again.

"Is Tess home?" Cody asked.

"I think so," I said. "But this isn't a good time to come over. Catch her later at the pool, okay?"

"Okay," Cody said. "See you."

I watched him skate away. Cody had the most gigantic crush on Tess. Everyone knew it, too. Everyone except Tess! For some reason, she didn't notice that he hung around her every second he could.

I opened the big gate that led from the street into our courtyard. Then I kicked off my skates, propped up my surfboard, and headed inside the house.

Tess was in the kitchen, making breakfast.

"Tess," I said, "we've got to talk."

"What's up?" my sister asked, her blue eyes widening. She was wearing her pajamas. Her blond hair was piled on top of her head, just like mine.

"It's Dad," I said.

Tess set a bowl of corn flakes, a pitcher of milk, and a glass of juice onto a tray. "What about him?"

"He's a mess," I said. "Haven't you noticed?"

Tess nodded. "He's a little bummed out these days," she said. "He misses Mom."

"A *little*?" I said. "Are you kidding? His favorite color is black! His favorite weather is cloudy with a chance of thunderstorms!"

"He's not *that* bad," Tess said.

"Oh, yeah? Remember what he said when I asked him what he wanted for his birthday? He said, 'Nothing. I don't feel like celebrating.'"

"That *was* a bad day," Tess agreed.

"We've got to get him out there, and meeting people," I said. "If he can't get himself moving again, it's up to us to help out, right?"

Tess nodded. "Right." She picked up the breakfast tray and headed for Dad's studio. We knew that's where we'd find him. That's where he *always* was these days.

"Breakfast!" Tess announced as we hurried into the sunny space.

Dad was standing over one of his metal sculptures, staring at it with bloodshot eyes.

"Morning, Monster. Morning, Munchkin," he

said. Those are his nicknames for me and Tess. "Come here." He opened his arms to give us hugs.

My dad is usually pretty good-looking—for a grown-up. But right then he could have passed for some other species. His wavy brown hair was covered with dust. His pants, too. And he hadn't shaved in a long time, either.

I hugged him anyway. "We brought you breakfast, Daddy," I announced.

"Breakfast?" He frowned. "It's morning already?"

"You've been working all night again, haven't you?" Tess asked him.

Okay, that's it, I thought. We were getting him out of the house today—no matter what!

"Dad, you missed some killer waves this morning," I said, trying to perk up his interest. "Six footers. How come you never go surfing anymore?"

"Oh, I don't know," he answered. "I guess I just haven't felt like it."

"But Dad, you haven't felt like doing *anything* with us lately," Tess said.

He flinched and looked guilty. "Okay, so what do you want to do today?" he asked. He tried to sound as if he was ready for anything.

"How about meeting us for ice cream?" I suggested. "This afternoon? After we go to the pool?"

"Yeah," Tess added. "At Van Go's."

"Van Go's?" Dad asked.

Uh-oh, I thought, holding my breath. *That's the place on the boardwalk where Dad took Mom on their first date. I hope that doesn't make him upset.*

Dad swallowed hard, and nodded. "Okay, sure."

"That'll be great!" I said, relaxing a little. "Remember how we used to hang out there all the time?"

"And remember how Autumn, the owner, even named a special sundae after us?" Tess went on.

"With cookie-dough ice cream!" I said. "And marshmallow sauce!"

"And whipped cream and nuts!" Tess shouted. "And three spoons!"

Whoops. There went Dad's face. When Mom was alive, that's what we used to get every time. That sundae—with *four* spoons.

"Listen, you girls go for ice cream without me," Dad told us. "I've got a lot of work to do." He put on his welding visor, and went back to sculpting.

This was even worse than I thought. Tess and I were going to have to come up with a more drastic plan than ice cream to get Dad back into action.

Luckily, I knew exactly where we should start!

CHAPTER TWO

"Now what are we going to do?" Tess whispered as we walked out of Dad's studio.

"Don't worry, I have an idea," I answered. "But we can't talk here. I'll tell you at the pool."

I glanced at the clock. Tess and I were due at the swim club for diving practice in twenty minutes.

I don't know how I got roped onto the diving team. I'm not a great diver. Actually, I'm the worst on the team. Tess is another story. She's awesome! She can even do dives with twists in them.

We put on our bathing suits, packed up our gear, and started to leave. We didn't get very far, though. Just as we were heading out, Nigel walked in the door. He was always letting himself in—as if he lived in our house.

Nigel is Dad's agent. He sells Dad's sculptures for him—and takes some of the money as payment.

"Hi, sweeties," he said with a fake British accent.

In real life he's probably from the Bronx or something. That's part of the reason I don't really trust Nigel. How do I know what he's saying isn't as phony as his accent?

Anyway, he was wearing an expensive-looking suit, sunglasses, and Italian loafers. I glanced out the door and spotted his new Range Rover parked outside the gate.

"Hey, Nigel," I said. "How come Dad is still driving his old Cutlass, and *you* get a new car every few months?"

Nigel shrugged. "I have to look successful for our clients, don't I?" he replied. Then he peered toward the studio. "So how is our favorite moody artist?"

"Lousy," Tess answered. "All he does is work."

Nigel beamed. "*That's* what I like to hear!"

He doesn't care about Dad, I thought as we slipped out the door and through the gate. *All he cares about is making money.* "There's something fishy about that guy," I told my sister.

"No kidding," Tess agreed. "All you need is mayo and he'd make a perfect tuna sandwich!"

When we got to the pool, most of the kids on the diving team were already practicing. Tess took a quick swim for a warm-up. Then she climbed the ladder to the three-meter board and did a forward one-and-a-half dive with a half twist.

"Awesome!" Cody cheered from the side.

"Your turn, Emily," our coach, Brad Thomas, called from across the pool.

My heart instantly started thumping. Not because I was afraid to dive or anything. It was because of *Brad*.

Brad is about the most perfect specimen of hunk I've ever seen in my life. He's six feet two, with sandy blond hair, rippling muscles, and blue eyes you could drown in.

I knew I didn't stand a chance with him. I mean, he *is* a college freshman. And I'm only in the eighth grade. But it doesn't hurt to dream, right?

"Come on, Emily!" Brad called. "Let's see an inward pike. You can do it."

I climbed up the ladder and onto the board. *Anything for the Westside Squids diving team*, I thought. *And Brad*.

My heart was still pounding, but I tried to stay focused. I didn't want to make a complete fool of myself in front of Brad.

I walked to the end of the board and turned around. Then I sprang off the board backwards, piked quickly and threw my legs in the air. I splashed into the water.

My dive wasn't perfect, but it wasn't a whale impersonation, either. I swam to the edge of the pool.

"Not bad," Brad told me. "Much better."

"Thanks, Brad," I said, staring at him dreamily.

He smiled and leaned over to give me a hand out of the water. "I've never trained a more beautiful and talented diver," he murmured suavely. "Can I take you to the next eighth grade dance?"

"Of course, Brad," I answered. "Pick me up at seven-thirty."

In my dreams. *TWEEEEET!* The sound of Brad's whistle snapped me out of that one. Fast.

"Listen up," he said, gathering all of the Squids around him. "We've all got a major diving meet coming up. Against our big rivals, the Palos Verdes Swim Club. So we need everyone to put in as much practice time as possible. Okay?"

Everyone nodded.

"Okay, take a little break right now," Brad said. "Then we'll start working on some new dives."

I stood there, watching Brad walk away.

Tess headed over to a picnic table at the end of the pool. "Yo! Love struck!" she called to me. "Come on!"

"Shhhh!" I said, hurrying over.

Tess rolled her eyes. "You should concentrate as much on your diving as you do on the diving instructor," she told me. "If you did, we might have

10

a chance to win the regionals."

"I can't help it." I turned to look at Brad again. "Isn't he gorgeous?"

"He's not her type," Cody answered, walking up.

Cody's not on the team, but he hangs out at the pool all the time. Guess why?

"Oh?" Tess answered. "What exactly *is* my type?"

Cody shrugged and almost blushed. "Never mind." He reached into his jeans pocket and pulled out two concert tickets. "Check this out," he said. "Two tickets to the No Doubt concert for next weekend. My dad worked on their last album, so I got backstage passes!"

Cody's dad was a musician. He played guitar for a bunch of different rock groups.

"That's so cool!" Tess cried. "My favorite band!"

Cody's face lit up. I knew that was the reaction he was hoping for. "Good," he said. "I thought one of you might be up for it."

One of us? Duh! He wanted Tess to go with him—not me.

But Tess shook her head. "Sorry. Our dad won't let us go to concerts without a responsible adult," she explained.

"Hey, no problem," Cody said. "My live-in babysitter will be there. She's eighteen."

"She said *responsible*," I reminded him. "Your baby-sitter used to be a groupie. Your dad met her on tour!"

Cody quickly changed the subject. "Hey, anyone need a hot dog?" he asked. "I'm starving."

Tess and I shook our heads. "Not while we're diving," I said.

"Oh. Yeah. Well, I'll catch you later," he said.

"So what's your big plan to bring Dad back to earth?" Tess asked me as Cody headed off to the snack bar.

"You know how I said Dad needs to meet more people? Well, I really think we need to find him a date," I said.

Tess stared at me. "A *date*?"

"I know it seems weird, but somebody has to help him. And maybe a girlfriend will cheer him up!" I reached into my backpack and pulled out a newspaper. "So—let's go through the personals. And answer one of the ads."

Tess thought about that for a second. Then she gave me a nod of approval. "Let's do it!" she said.

I spread the newspaper out on the table in front of us. "Okay, here's one," I said, pointing.

We both read it. "SWF, 30's, n/s, ISO SM, B&B for R&M."

"What is this?" Tess complained. "We need a code book to figure these things out!"

I laughed. "No we don't. It's easy." I translated for her. "Single white female in her thirties, non-smoker, in search of single male, brown hair and brown eyes—that's the B&B part—for romance and monogamy."

"Wow. You're good," Tess said admiringly.

"Well, you have to read between the lines," I told her. "But let's circle that one. She sounds good."

"And Dad's perfect for her," Tess agreed. "He even has brown hair and brown eyes."

I kept reading through the ads, circling the ones that sounded good.

A few minutes later Cody came back with a hot dog.

"Hey!" I complained. "You're getting mustard all over our newspaper!"

He peered over my shoulder. "You're reading the personals?" he asked. "Don't you know that people who place those ads are weird?"

"We're trying to find our dad a girlfriend," I explained.

"Oh. Well, that's easy," Cody said. "Your dad's a famous artist. He must have all kinds of babes hanging around him."

"He has plenty of groupies," Tess said.

"But he hates all those women who hang around him in the gallery," I added. "We need someone like Mom was. Someone smart and pretty, who's independent—but still likes being taken care of once in a while."

"Hey, I know!" Cody's eyes lit up. "My dad's record company got him a billboard over on Sunset Boulevard to advertise his last CD. Girls were mobbing the streets when they saw it."

A billboard! Tess and I looked at each other.

"I'm liking this," Tess said.

"Me, too," I agreed. "A personal ad on a billboard! The whole city would see it! We'd get tons of answers!"

"Right." Cody flashed his dark eyes at Tess.

She smiled back at him. "Cody, you're the best!"

I had to agree. A billboard for Dad was an amazing idea! It was the perfect way to find him the perfect girlfriend.

There was just one question.

How were we going to do it?

CHAPTER THREE

"Is he asleep?" I peered into Dad's studio. It was after midnight. But at least he had finally stopped working. He was zonked on the couch—and snoring.

"Oh, great!" Tess cracked. "I can see it all now. Single white dad, snorer, seeks hard-of-hearing woman for romance and nasal fun."

"We won't put *that* on his billboard!" I assured her. "Come on. Let's get out of here!"

The two of us crept through the house and into the courtyard. We were both dressed in black so it would be hard to see us in the dark.

We grabbed two huge bags of gear and hurried to meet Cody on the corner of our street. He had called a cab to take us to Sunset Boulevard.

Luckily, the driver didn't ask any questions. When he dropped us off, Cody told him to come back and get us in exactly one hour.

"There it is!" Cody said as the cab drove off. He pointed up at a gigantic billboard. It was totally blank—except for the words: YOUR AD HERE.

"Talk about maximum exposure!" Tess exclaimed. "Everyone on the strip will see this!"

I stared at the sign and gulped. "It's perfect," I agreed. "But it's so...high!" I was starting to get second thoughts about climbing up there.

"Don't think about that," Tess said. "Just pretend it's a diving board."

Easy for her to say. She dove from the three-meter board all the time.

I was scared, but I took a deep breath, and we went for it anyway.

Cody was great. He grabbed a bag of gear and climbed all the way to the top of the billboard.

Tess and I stopped when we reached the cat-walk. That's the platform that runs in front of the bottom edge of the sign.

"Don't look down," Tess warned me.

We stripped off our layer of black clothes. Underneath, we had on white T-shirts and white overalls. Now we blended in with the billboard.

Cody lowered the buckets of paint from the top of the sign using ropes. Then we got to work. With wide brushes, we painted the first part of the message. It said: "He's single. He's handsome. He's cool to the Max!" That last part was my idea because our dad's name is Max.

Then we changed the part where it said: YOUR AD HERE. We painted over the Y and added a D in front of the word AD. When we were done, it said: OUR DAD HERE!

Then we painted the rest of the message. It said, "Interested? Write to Max Tyler at 50 Surf St., Venice."

The best part was the photograph. We'd given Cody a picture of our dad, and he'd had a gigantic photocopy made. We pasted it up there so everyone could see what Dad looked like.

It was a lot of work, but we were proud of it.

"I'm wiped out," Tess moaned as we finally climbed down from the billboard.

"No kidding," I said, yawning.

I checked my watch. Two A.M.! The cab would be here any minute.

But we had done it. We had put Dad's name, address, and picture on a billboard. Now half the women in California would know he was available.

"Dad will *have* to get some good dates out of this," Tess said. "Won't he?"

"I hope so," I said. I thought about how super sad Dad had been lately and shook my head. "This billboard has to work. It just *has* to!"

CHAPTER FOUR

BZZZZZZZ!

"No," I moaned. "Not the alarm already." I slammed my hand on the snooze button and pulled my pillow over my head.

But the buzzer kept ringing over and over. It's the door, I realized. I glanced at the blue, glow-in-the-dark alarm clock I shared with my sister. It was only eight A.M.—on a Sunday.

BZZZZZ! BZZZ-BZZZ-BZZZ!

"I'll get it," I told Tess. I dragged myself out of bed and headed downstairs.

But Dad was already there. "Hi, Monster," he said.

"Morning, Daddy." I followed him and watched him open the gate.

Dad's mouth dropped open when he saw the woman standing outside. So did mine.

She was totally wild-looking. Her tight black dress, leather jacket, and studded leather boots were only part of her look. Her makeup was painted on as thick as frosting. And her hair was like straw. Dyed red. I *guess* you'd call it red.

"Uh, wrong house," Dad said. He thought she was one of Cody's dad's groupies. "The musician lives three doors down."

The woman shook her head and smiled with big teeth. "I'm looking for *you*, Dad." She pointed a long fingernail at him.

"Excuse me?" Dad asked.

"Well, I realize this is a little crazy—me just showing up like this," she explained. "But I'm not good with letters."

Dad kept standing there, staring.

"What's going on?" Tess whispered to me, coming up in her pajamas.

I wasn't sure—but I was starting to wonder. Did this woman see our billboard?

"You two must be the artists," the woman said. She pointed at Tess and me.

Yep, I thought. *She saw the billboard.*

"No, no, *I'm* the artist," Dad said. "They're my daughters. Who are *you*?"

"Well, I'm *interested*," the woman said, winking.

Tess and I exchanged looks.

"Yes!" Tess burst out, giving me a high five.

Dad spun around. "Will someone tell me what this is all about?" he said, trying to sound calm.

"It's the billboard," the woman at the gate explained. "What else?"

"Billboard?" Dad threw up his hands. "Someone better start giving me the four-one-one—and fast."

"You mean he doesn't know?" the woman asked. Her eyes opened wide. "Wow."

"Uh, I think we'd better *show* you, Dad," Tess said. "Come on, Emily. Let's get dressed."

"Show me what?" Dad asked. He turned to the woman and tried to be polite. "You'll excuse us, won't you?" he said.

Then he slammed the gate in her face.

Tess and I didn't want to spoil the surprise, so we didn't answer any of Dad's questions. We just asked him to please drive us to Sunset Boulevard.

When we pulled up, there was a crowd of people standing on the sidewalk. Most of them were women. They were staring up at the sign.

And TV news reporters were interviewing them!

"Wow!" Tess cried. "Look, Dad—you're famous!"

"There it is, Daddy," I said. I pointed out the car window. "Your very own billboard!"

Dad stumbled as he got out of the car. He looked at the billboard. Then at us. Then back at the billboard again. "You girls did this?"

"Isn't it the best?" Tess said, excited. "Look!" She

pointed to all the women who were copying down our address from the sign. "They all want *you*!"

Dad started to say something. But a swarm of TV reporters suddenly spotted us. In seconds the whole mob surrounded us.

I recognized Kitty Buxbaum, the anchorwoman from one of the local TV stations. She was standing nearest to our dad.

A cameraman turned on the lights and starting taping. "You're on, Kitty," he said.

"Here in Los Angeles," Kitty began, "people will do *anything* to get noticed. I'm on Sunset Boulevard with Billboard Dad, the man who put a personal ad on a billboard. Tell me, Dad, what made you so desperate that you decided to take out an entire billboard for yourself?"

"Frankly, I have to say I find this whole thing pretty embarrassing," Dad mumbled.

"He didn't do it," Tess explained quickly. "It was *our* idea."

"Oh, my goodness," Kitty said. "These must be your daughters. And they're *twins*! Are you telling me you *girls* did all of this for your father?"

"That's right." Tess beamed. "It was all my idea."

Actually, it was Cody's idea, I wanted to say. But who cared about that now? We were on TV!

"So tell me, girls," Kitty Buxbaum went on, "what made you do this for your father?"

"He's single, he's good-looking, and he has a lot to offer a woman," Tess said. She smiled straight at the camera.

"He's awesome," I added. "But he's too nice to go around telling people that. So we said it for him."

Kitty smiled. "Well, there you have it," she said into the camera. "From the mouths of babes."

Kitty turned to Dad again. "Well, Billboard Dad, you certainly are lucky to have two such creative daughters. We'll be following this story closely to see how it turns out!"

Then the camera lights went off. Kitty didn't even say goodbye to us or anything. She just marched off toward her TV truck and drove away.

Dad didn't say a word. I was beginning to feel a little nervous now. I could tell Tess was, too.

"So? Do you like it?" she asked Dad.

I held my breath. I thought our billboard was the greatest. But Dad didn't look so sure.

"I think we'll talk about this when we get home," he said, steering my sister and me toward the car. "In *private*."

Uh-oh. That did not sound good!

CHAPTER FIVE

Tess and I were nervous all the way home.

See, our dad almost never blows up at us when he's mad. He just gets really, really quiet. So the fact that we rode home in total silence wasn't exactly the best sign.

But even if Tess and I were in big trouble, I was still glad about what we'd done. Dad's billboard was the greatest.

The light was flashing on our answering machine when we got home. So Dad didn't get a chance to launch into a long talk with us right away. He had to call the billboard company back to explain everything.

While he was on the phone, Nigel walked in and made himself at home, like always.

Dad finally got off the phone. "Well, it seems that the billboard company will not be pressing charges," he said.

"What billboard company?" Nigel asked.

Dad ignored him. "Luckily, they love the free

publicity that they're getting."

"*What* publicity?" Nigel demanded.

"They're not going to take it down, are they?" Tess asked.

"Yeah!" I said. "What about all the women who are going to answer the ad?"

"*What* women?" Nigel snapped.

Ha, ha, I thought. I loved seeing Nigel left out.

"Girls, girls." Dad motioned for us to sit with him on the couch. "Listen, I know you only meant to help. But if I want to go out with a woman—which I *don't*—I'll find my own date, okay? And not by putting up a billboard over Sunset Strip!"

"Fine, Daddy," I said. "But how? You hardly ever leave the studio anymore."

Tess nodded. "You don't hang out with your old friends," she said. "You don't even do anything with us anymore."

"What's wrong with *that?*" Nigel argued.

Dad shot Nigel an irritated look.

Luckily, Nigel took the hint. He walked over to the kitchen and poured himself a cold drink.

Dad's face softened when he looked back at Tess and me. "Okay," he said. "Maybe you're right. Maybe I do need to change things a little bit. But that billboard was not a good plan. And I don't even want to *think* about how you girls were up there, painting it. In the middle of the night!"

"We were careful," Tess said meekly. "And we weren't alone. Cody came with us."

"Oh, great!" Dad rolled his eyes.

I tried to get back to the main topic. "So how are we going to change things around here?" I asked. "I mean, are you going to start dating again?"

"No!" Nigel blurted out from the kitchen.

Dad shot him another glare.

"I mean, you want to stay focused on your work, don't you, Max?" Nigel added.

"We'll talk about this later," Dad said, sighing. "Aren't you girls late for diving practice?"

I glanced at the clock. Whoa! We were supposed to be at the pool twenty minutes ago!

Tess and I raced to get our bathing suits.

I was feeling kind of happy inside. Our billboard ad was a hit. Dad wasn't all that mad. And he was at least *thinking* about dating.

There was only one person who could ruin the whole thing. Nigel.

If Dad's greedy agent had his way, he'd keep Dad single for the rest of his life!

CHAPTER SIX

By the time we got to the pool, the other kids on the team had already warmed up.

"Where were you?" Brad asked us. He sounded grumpy.

What a hunk! I thought. *He's even cute when he's mad!*

But he didn't let us answer. "Never mind. We've got a lot of work to do," he said. "Listen, Tess—we want to beat Palos Verdes at the regionals, right?"

"Definitely," Tess said, nodding.

"Well, the meet is coming up in a month," Brad went on. "And I just found out that their team has added a new dive. A reverse pike—off the high platform."

Uh-oh, I thought. My sister was an ace diver. But even *she* didn't dive off the high board!

"I don't know," Tess said slowly. "I'll give it a shot."

"That's my girl." Brad flashed her his killer smile and walked away.

My heart sank. "He called you his girl!"

Tess just shook her head. "Get over yourself, Emily."

Brad blew his whistle so everyone would get back to work.

Tess shivered a little. I saw her staring up at the platform. She took a deep breath and headed toward it.

I huddled with Julianne and Kristen—two of the other divers on our team.

"Do you think she can do it?" Kristen asked.

"We've got four more weeks." I said, trying to sound casual. But inside, I was almost as nervous as Tess. I knew everyone was counting on her.

We all watched Tess climb the ladder to the high platform. When she got to the top, she stared down at the water.

"Just pretend it's like the *low* dive," Brad called to her. "Only higher."

"Yeah," Tess called back. "Much higher."

"Concentrate," Brad said. "Remember: Nice, clean entry."

Tess put her arms out in the air. Then she launched herself off the platform. Her pike was great—but she made a loud, messy splash as she went into the water.

Everyone on the team groaned in sympathy.

"Terrible," Tess said as she shot up out of the water.

"Don't worry," Brad said. "We've got time to work on it."

Tess climbed out of the water and headed straight back to the board.

Just then some kid about our age rolled past us on a skateboard. He practically ran over our feet!

"Hey!" Julianne yelled. "Can't you read?" She pointed at the sign on the fence around the pool. It said: NO SKATEBOARDS.

But the kid ignored her. He flipped up his skateboard, changed directions, and skated back toward us.

What a creep! I thought, checking him out. He had bleached hair, three earrings in one ear, something pierced through his eyebrow, and a bad attitude. "Who is that, anyway?" I asked.

"Some new kid," Kristen answered. "His name is Ryan. I hear he's from Holly*weird*."

Ryan started to make another turn on his board. But he was watching Tess. Just as she dived into the pool, his board hit a bump and...*SPLASH!*

He flew through the air, head over heels, right into the water!

In a flash Brad dived into the pool to save Ryan.

Ryan squirmed to get free. "Let go of me, college boy!" he shouted. "I'm fine!"

Everyone laughed—except Tess. "How would *you* like it if someone laughed because you fell into the water?" she asked.

But we all just laughed harder. Except Ryan, of course.

"Well, it *was* sort of funny," Tess admitted.

Ryan frowned. "Yeah. Hilarious," he said. "About as funny as your dive. Are you going to dive that way at the regionals?"

Tess's face flushed red. "You think you can do better?" she snapped.

Ryan nodded and marched straight over to the high platform. We all stared as Ryan got ready to dive—in his clothes!

"You know what?" Julianne whispered. "I heard he goes to some special school for problem kids."

"I heard he got kicked out of there!" Kristen shot back.

"Yeah? Well *I* heard he did time at Juvenile Hall," Julianne added.

Tess looked nervous, watching him on the high board. As if she was afraid he might show her up.

And here's the awful part. He *did*.

He nailed a perfect reverse pike. Even with pants on, he hardly made a splash going into the water!

Brad raced over to the edge of the pool. "You just made the diving team!" he told Ryan.

Ryan shrugged and shook his head. "I've got better things to do than be on your stupid team," he said.

"No way," Brad told him. "Let's talk about this." He followed Ryan down to the other end of the pool.

I glanced at Tess's face. It had turned from red to white. She really looked upset.

What's she so worried about? I wondered. Okay—maybe now she was the *second* best diver on the Squids. But there were six places on the team. If Ryan joined, Tess wouldn't get bumped off. Only the worst person on the team would get bumped off.

Wait a minute. I let out a gasp. *That's me!*

CHAPTER SEVEN

BZZZZZ! The doorbell woke us up again the next morning.

I leaped out of bed, excited. "Maybe it's another woman for Dad!" I told Tess. "Come on!"

Tess climbed out of bed, yawning.

But when we got to the front gate, it was only Charlie, the mailman. He was standing there with two huge bags of mail. "Is your dad home?" he asked, dropping the sacks with a thud.

"Right here!" Dad called, coming to see what was happening.

"Hey, Mr. Tyler," Charlie said. "I've got quite a bit of mail for you."

Tess and I looked at each other.

The ad! All that mail had to be for Billboard Dad!

"I've got two more bags outside, too," Charlie said. He went out to his truck and brought them in.

"I can't believe this," Dad said, shaking his head.

"By the way," Charlie said to Tess and me. "I saw

you on the news. Nice job, girls. We're with you!"

"Wow!" I cried.

Tess started dragging one of the bags of letters into the living room. I grabbed another, and Dad brought the other two.

"There must be a million letters here!" Tess cried.

"*Two* million!" I guessed, pulling open one of the sacks.

Dad plopped on the couch and watched us open some letters.

I held one up. It was written on pink paper and smelled of perfume. "This one even *smells* romantic," I reported.

"This one sent a bribe!" Tess cried. She pulled a ten-dollar bill out of the envelope.

"Hey, look," I said, ripping open another letter. "Here's a picture." I showed it to Dad.

"That's a cat," he said.

I frowned at the picture. It was upside down. "No, it just looks like a cat," I said, turning the picture around. "See?"

"Oh, my goodness, you're right!" Dad said in horror. "It must have been the whiskers that threw me."

Okay, so maybe she wasn't the woman of his

dreams. But they couldn't *all* be losers—could they?

"Dad, aren't you at least a *little* bit curious?" Tess asked. "I mean, some of these women sound really great."

"Oh, yeah?" Dad muttered.

"Look, this one's a doctor," Tess told him. "And here's a concert cellist."

"I've got a fashion model!" I exclaimed, waving a picture around. "Don't you want to be seen with a killer babe?"

Dad still didn't look thrilled.

"Come on, Dad. You promised," I begged him. "You said things would have to change around here, right?"

He shrugged. "I guess so."

"Please, Dad," Tess said. "Just go on a couple of dates and see how things work out."

He was weakening, I could tell. A little more pleading should do it. "Please?" I begged. "For us?"

"Pleeease?" Tess added.

"All right, I tell you what," Dad said finally. "I will go out on three dates. And that's it."

"Seven," Tess replied.

"Five," Dad offered.

"Sold!" I cried, jumping up to cheer.

"Just remember," Dad added quickly. "I'm only

doing this because I love you two very much. After five dates you will leave me alone—right? Is that understood?"

We both nodded quickly. We knew not to push our luck.

"Okay," Dad said. "I'll look through the letters."

"We'll help!" Tess offered.

Dad rolled his eyes. "Oh, thanks. Just what I need!"

"Come on, Dad," I argued. "You're not going to have all the fun alone, are you?"

"That *is* what dating is supposed to be about," he said. "A man and a woman go out together. *Alone*."

Tess and I both pouted big-time.

"Okay." He gave in. "But remember: five dates—that's it!"

CHAPTER EIGHT

"Dad, *no!* Not *that* tie!" Tess cried two nights later.

Dad was getting ready to go out on his first date. Tess and I were so psyched. I mean, this could be it! The beginning of a whole new life—for Dad *and* for us.

But my sister was right. The tie Dad was wearing was at least ten years old. Totally hideous and out of style.

"Whoa! Wait here," I said. I raced toward the office that Nigel sometimes used. Nigel spent big bucks on his clothes. And he always kept some extra ties in the desk. I grabbed a cool silver one and ran back to Dad's room. "Try this one," I told him.

Dad put it on, and we gave him the once-over.

"Okay. You'll do," Tess announced. We walked him to the gate. "Have fun!"

"Thanks, girls," Dad said. He even sounded like he meant it. Maybe he was actually looking forward to this date. "Uh, don't wait up for me, okay?"

"Are you kidding?" I answered. "We'll be up. We want to hear every detail!"

Dad groaned, but he didn't argue. He headed out the door with a nervous look on his face.

Hey, who can blame him? I thought. He hadn't been in the dating scene for years.

Tess and I made a bowl of microwave popcorn. Then we settled down to watch a movie. We had rented three, just in case. Who knew how late Dad would be out? But halfway into the first flick, I heard the front gate open.

I glanced at the clock on the VCR. He had only been gone an hour. "Uh-oh," I said. "Dad's back."

"Too soon." Tess's face drooped.

We both leaped off the couch and ran to meet him.

"What happened?" Tess demanded.

Dad shook his head and slumped into a chair. "Disaster."

"What went wrong?" I asked.

Dad shrugged. "This was the kindergarten teacher. The one you picked, Emily."

Uh-oh, I thought. *My fault.* "She sounded good on paper," I told him. "She said she loved children."

"Oh, she likes children, all right," Dad said. "She

talked baby talk all night. But that wasn't the worst part. She actually reached across the table and wiped my mouth with a napkin. Then she cut my meat for me!"

"Okay," I said. "So the teacher didn't work out. But you've still got four to go, right?"

Tess and I decided to check out what was *really* happening on Dad's dates. That's why we followed him the next time.

We tailed Dad to an Italian restaurant called Garibaldi's—just a few blocks from our house. And we spied from behind a potted palm tree.

"What does she look like?" Tess whispered.

I peeked out. Dad's date was wearing a black veil that covered almost all of her face. I could tell Dad didn't know what to say to her.

Finally we heard him say, "You have lovely eyes."

That was about it for Date Number Two.

Luckily, Dad took all of his dates to Garibaldi's. That meant Tess and I could spy from behind the potted palm again.

Date Number Three talked about ear wax all through dinner. Honest. And Date Number Four whined about her old boyfriend all night.

Date Number Five looked like she might work

out. She was a pretty French woman with great legs and a slinky red dress. But when Dad saw her hairy armpits, he got grossed out.

"Oh, well, girls," he said when he came home from the last date. "We tried. But I guess this just isn't the way to find the kind of woman I'd be looking for. *If* I were looking."

"Oh, come on, Dad!" I begged. "One more try."

"We should have made it seven dates," Tess argued.

"A deal's a deal," Dad said firmly. "And that's final."

"But we've still got a whole bag full of letters we didn't even read," I said. "There's got to be someone in there for you! How come you won't give it a shot?"

Dad just shook his head. End of story.

I was so bummed. There were still thousands of women out there who still wanted a chance with him. And Dad was just giving up!

But I knew not to argue with him anymore. He looked pretty disappointed about the whole thing himself.

"Come on, Emily," Tess said. "We've got early diving practice tomorrow. Let's go to bed."

I follow her upstairs. But when we got to the top

of the staircase, I heard Dad talking to himself.

"Why *don't* I just give it a shot?" Dad said.

"Hey, Tess," I whispered. "Look."

We peeked over the railing and saw Dad take one of the letters out of the mailbag. Only instead of reading it, he crumpled it up. Then he aimed at the basketball hoop that we have rigged up in our living room.

"If it goes in, I go out on a date with her," he said. "If not, I quit." He arched his wrist and shot.

"Missed!" Tess said, disappointed.

I felt terrible, too. I wanted Dad to make that shot so badly. He just *had* to find someone who could cheer him up.

Then I saw Dad reach into the mailbag again. I poked Tess in the ribs. "Look! He's trying again!" I whispered.

"Okay, one more try," he mumbled.

He aimed. And shot.

And missed again.

"More arch!" Tess coached him softly.

"Keep trying, Dad," I prayed softly.

He did. The only problem was, he was totally off his game. He tried one letter after another. But none of them went into the basket. By now, the living room floor was totally covered in crumpled pieces of paper from the mailbag.

There were only two letters left.

"I can't watch," I told Tess, covering my eyes.

"I will marry this woman," Dad said. He was holding the next-to-last letter.

I held my breath.

"It's up," Tess reported.

"And?" I still didn't look.

"And…it's bad," she said, her voice dropping in disappointment.

So that was it. Dad had only one letter left. And he had already missed about two hundred times.

What were the chances that he'd actually sink the very last one?

CHAPTER NINE

"Oh, well," we heard Dad mutter. "I never liked dating, anyway."

Tess and I grabbed each other's hands and squeezed hard. We stared at the last letter that Dad was holding. Was he going to give up, without even trying to make it?

He sat there for a long time. Finally he crumpled the letter up into a ball. "Okay," Dad told himself. "The pressure is on." He leaned back, arched his arm up, and shot. *SWISH!*

"It went through!" Tess whispered. "I can't believe it."

"Yes!" I cried, punching the air.

Oops. Dad heard me. He looked up at us.

Tess and I ran downstairs to give him a hug.

"Dad! Are you going to call that woman?" I asked, jumping into his arms.

He frowned—for about two seconds. "How long have you girls been spying on me?" he asked.

"All four quarters," Tess answered. "And if you

ask me, you should have put in a sub from the bench a long time ago."

Dad laughed. "Okay, Monster, Munchkin. Run off to bed." He bent to pick up the winning letter— the one that had gone into the basket.

"Will you call her?" I asked again.

"Yes." He sighed. "I'll call her tomorrow."

It didn't take Dad long to set up the date. The woman's name was Debbie. Dad said she sounded nice on the phone. They made plans to meet Sunday afternoon at the art museum.

Good, I thought. *That's much better than going to dinner at Garibaldi's.* After all, Dad was an artist. He'd be much more comfortable in a museum than a restaurant. It was the perfect place to find out if he and Debbie had anything in common.

"Dad, promise to tell us everything?" Tess asked as he was going out the door.

"You'll get information on a need-to-know basis," he said.

"Hey!" I called after him. "This whole billboard ad was our idea, remember?"

"You don't need to remind me," Dad said. "Wish me luck."

Of course Tess and I weren't going to leave anything up to luck. We waited a few minutes, and then followed him out the door!

When we got to the museum, Dad was already sitting on a bench in the sculpture garden. Lots of people were walking around, looking at the art. Tess and I found a spot, around a corner, where we could watch Dad without being seen.

A few minutes later a beautiful woman with wavy blond hair sat down next to him.

"There's his date!" I whispered to Tess.

"She's very pretty," Tess said. "And look, Dad's smiling. I think he likes her!"

Wow, I thought. *Wouldn't it be incredible if this actually works out?*

"Let's get closer," Tess said. "We need to hear what they're saying."

I nodded. We moved to a better hiding spot, right behind a marble column.

"Yes, I'm a sculptor," Dad was saying. "But I don't actually have my work in this museum yet."

"Don't feel bad," the woman replied. "I think you have to be dead to get your work in here."

"Oh." Dad laughed. "Then I guess I can wait a few more years."

Tess nudged me. "I think he's having a good time!"

"Shhh," I said. "He'll hear us!"

43

"So you said you came here with a friend—who's on a blind date?" Dad asked.

"That's right," the woman answered. "My best friend actually wrote that guy on TV. You know, Billboard Dad? I'm just here in case she needs to be bailed out."

Oh, no! I thought. *He's falling for the wrong woman!*

Where was his real date?

"I'm curious," Dad said. His cheeks were a little red. "Why didn't *you* answer that ad?"

"Because love doesn't happen that way," the woman said. "You can't just find it on a billboard."

Just then, someone tapped me on the back. I jumped.

"Excuse me," a woman said behind me. "You girls were on TV, weren't you? Aren't you Billboard Dad's kids?"

Tess nodded and smiled. "That's us!"

"Well, where's your father?" she asked. "I'm his date!"

Tess and I glanced at each other and then at the woman. Debbie. That was her name, wasn't it?

She was pretty enough—but she didn't seem as *special* as the one Dad was talking to.

But, hey, I thought. *Dad made a date with her.* Of

course he was going to keep it. And Debbie did seem to be a nice person.

We quickly led her over to Dad and introduced her. "Dad! Look!" I said, trying to sound excited. "We found your date!"

Debbie gave Dad a slightly hurt look. "For a minute there, I thought you stood me up."

"Sorry," Dad said. "I was talking to your friend. I didn't know you were waiting."

"*You're* Billboard Dad?" the pretty woman said. She sounded shockèd.

"Max, actually," Dad said. He reached out to shake hands.

"Brooke," the woman introduced herself.

Their eyes locked. It looked like instant love.

"And I'm Debbie," the other woman spoke up. "Remember me?"

"Oh, sorry," Dad said again.

Debbie could obviously see that Brooke liked Dad. And that Dad liked Brooke. So she said, "Hey, listen, why don't you two have lunch together?"

Talk about a good friend! I said to myself.

"Really? Thanks," Brooke said, giving Debbie a hug.

After that, Dad drove me and Tess home. He *thought* he was getting rid of us so he and Brooke could go out to lunch alone. Of course Tess and I followed him on foot. We knew where he was going. Garibaldi's. Where else?

He got his regular table there. And we took our hiding spot behind the potted palm tree.

"What's she saying?" Tess asked me.

"She's telling him that she's an eye doctor," I answered. "And he told her that she's beautiful."

"Cool," Tess said. "Let's give them a nudge."

"Okay," I agreed. "But how?"

Tess glanced around the restaurant. "Give me all the money you've got. I'll handle this." A minute later she came back with a sneaky grin on her face.

"What did you do?" I asked.

"I had the waiter send them desserts," she answered. "On the house. And I also had the flower lady bring a rose to their table. See?"

I peeked through the palm leaves. Sure enough, the flower lady was handing Brooke a beautiful long-stemmed red rose.

"Oh, for me?" Brooke said, beaming. She threw Dad a grateful smile. "Thank you," she said.

Dad looked confused. "Uh, sure. It was nothing, really."

"It's working!" I whispered to Tess. "She's getting all starry-eyed!"

46

"Let me see," Tess said. She poked me in the ribs to make me move over. Then, trying to get a better view, she stepped on my foot.

"Get off my foot!" I snapped, shoving her back.

"You've got your elbow in my stomach," Tess complained. She pushed me a little harder. I stumbled against the potted palm tree.

Uh-oh. It started leaning...leaning...

And then it crashed to the floor! Tess and I fell on top of it.

Everyone in the entire place stared at us.

Dad jumped up and ran over to see if we were all right. He tried to act really calm. Which meant we were in big trouble.

"Girls," he said pleasantly. "How nice to see you. We'll be talking about this later, won't we?"

Uh-oh. *Serious* trouble.

But I didn't care. Dad's date seemed to be a success. And he looked happy—really happy—for the first time in two years.

I wondered whether he would ask Brooke out again—and whether she would accept.

Of course. Why not? I thought.

What could possibly happen to mess up such a perfect match?

CHAPTER TEN

The next two weeks were the greatest. Dad and Brooke went out five more times. And Dad came home each night with a big, silly smile on his face. He was definitely falling in love.

Tess and I were happy, too. We spent every morning at the pool. Tess's platform dives were improving. She almost nailed her forward pike three times in a row.

And so far, that kid Ryan hadn't joined the Squids. My place on the team was still safe.

The only thing that wasn't clicking was my thing with Brad. Somehow, he hadn't figured out yet that we were meant for each other.

But I kept trying.

"Brad," I said one morning. "Don't you think my inward pike would improve faster if we spent more time on it—together?"

"You're doing just fine, Emily," he said. "Just remember to come out of the pike when you see the water. And don't be afraid. Reach for it."

"I'm totally fearless," I said, trying to impress him. I stared up into his big blue eyes.

"Hey, Fearless," a voice taunted me. "Better come out of your pike now—'cause here comes the water!"

An instant later I got hit in the back of the head with a stream of cold water. "Yeow!" I cried.

Brad laughed.

I whirled around and saw Ryan buzzing past me on his skateboard. He was squirting everyone with a giant Super Soaker.

"Watch where you're pointing that thing!" I yelled.

Ryan just laughed.

I started to go after him, but Tess grabbed my arm. "You were going to get wet in a minute, anyway," she said. "Let Ryan go. He's had a hard life. I heard he grew up in a foster home."

"So what?" I said. "He made me look like a dweeb in front of Brad!"

"Oh, Brad already knew you were a dweeb," Tess teased.

Ha, ha. Very funny. But I let it slide. Tess was right. Ryan was a total jerk. He wasn't worth the trouble it would take to get back at him.

A minute or so later Cody came over, carrying

some stuff under his arm. He handed it all to Tess.

"I got you this tape at the No Doubt concert," he said. "And an autographed T-shirt." He held it up for her. It was Tess's favorite color—purple.

"Wow, thanks, Cody!" she said. "That's awesome."

See what I mean? Life was almost perfect.

But then there was Nigel.

The more Dad went out with Brooke, the grumpier Nigel got. He hung around the house nonstop, ragging on Dad about how he should work more and go out less.

Then one day after diving practice, Nigel wasn't hanging around. But Dad was. With Brooke! He was giving her a tour of his studio.

"Let's listen in," Tess said. She pointed to the intercom in the living room, with a twinkle in her eye.

"How can we?" I asked her.

I mean, I knew how the intercom worked. There was one in the living room and another in Dad's studio. But you had to hold the button down to talk.

"I rigged it up this morning," Tess explained. "When Dad said he might bring Brooke over today."

"How?" I stared at the machine, amazed.

Tess shrugged. "Easy. Toothpick wedged on the

button, holding it down," she said.

"Cool!"

Tess and I huddled near the intercom in the living room. We pressed the button and leaned close to listen.

"My son would love this place," Brooke was saying. "You've got so many interesting tools."

Son? Tess and I looked at each other.

"She has a *kid*!" I said, shocked.

"I wonder how old he is?" Tess whispered.

"Shhh," I said. We went back to listening.

"He used to love to make things," Brooke went on. "Until he hit the rebellious stage. Now he just seems angry all the time."

"I think all kids start testing the limits at some point," Dad said.

"Yeah, I know," Brooke said. "And he's upset about his dad getting remarried."

"Well, bring him over sometime," Dad said. "I'd like him to meet my girls."

Wow! I thought. Dad and Brooke *must* be getting serious, if he wanted us to meet her son!

Whoa. What if they got really serious—like marriage?

"We could end up with a new mom," I murmured to Tess.

"And a brother!" Tess added.

This was a whole new idea. It had never occurred to us.

A voice right behind me made me jump. "Eavesdropping?" Nigel asked. "Naughty girls!"

Tess and I jerked away from the intercom.

Nigel was there again. Sneaking into our house like a thief.

"Well, nobody ever tells us anything!" Tess said. "So we *have* to listen in sometimes."

"Yeah," I chimed in. "How else are we going to find out what's going on?"

Nigel sniffed. "When I was a boy, we didn't have intercoms," he said. "We had to peek through key-holes and dig through the trash."

Yuck!

"Bye, Nigel," I said quickly as we hurried to our rooms.

A minute later I realized I had left my swimming gear in the living room. I started back to get it. And then I heard the intercom—still on.

"Hey, Tess!" I called in a loud whisper. "Look! Now Nigel's eavesdropping on Dad and Brooke!"

What a slime!

We sneaked up behind Nigel as quietly as we could. Then we both yelled, "Caught you!"

You should have seen him jump! He cleared his throat, embarrassed. "I see your dad is wasting his time with that woman again," he said. "The one who's keeping him away from his work."

"Dad has a right to have a life," Tess said.

"Fine," Nigel snapped. "But he has a huge show coming up in less than two weeks. He hasn't even started his masterpiece yet!"

"Don't you want Dad to be happy?" I asked.

Nigel leaned toward us. "Look, kiddies, if your father gets too *happy*, then his art might change. If his art changes, then it might not sell. And if it doesn't sell—poof! Say goodbye to your shiny little lifestyles." He sneered at us and walked out.

"*Our* shiny lifestyles?" I said. "*He's* the one driving the Range Rover!"

"And wearing a Rolex watch," Tess added.

"We've definitely got to keep an eye on Nigel," I told Tess. "Because if he has his way, Dad and Brooke will never stay together!"

CHAPTER ELEVEN

"Girls? Ready for your field trip with Brooke?" Dad called.

Tess and I hurried downstairs. "Shopping? Manicure? Beauty salon? Of course we're ready!" I exclaimed.

I grabbed a cardigan to match my pink sleeveless sweater. Then I kissed Dad goodbye and ran after Tess to Brooke's car.

"I wish our field trips for school were like this," Tess said as we drove toward the shopping strip.

"I know," Brooke said. "Instead, they take you to see how a sewage treatment plant works, right?"

Tess and I laughed. Brooke was cool. This was going to be a fabulous day!

"First stop—Emmanuel's," Brooke announced. She pulled up in front of the fanciest hair salon in Venice. It was one of those cool places where they let you change into a bathrobe to get your hair cut. And they bring you drinks the whole time.

Brooke had made three appointments for two

o'clock, so we didn't have to wait. We all got our hair done at the same time. We even had our toenails polished. It was awesome.

But the best part was just talking to Brooke. It was really fun getting to know her.

"So when do we get to meet your son?" Tess asked.

Brooke smiled. "How about tonight? He's going to come over to your house while your dad and I go out," she said. "You guys will get along great."

Wow, I thought. *Tonight! Things must really be going well between them.*

Mostly, I liked the idea of Dad and Brooke getting married. But having a new brother? That was a little weird.

I decided to change the subject. "Brooke, do you think a college guy could ever fall in love with a younger woman?"

"*Much* younger," Tess said. "Emily has a crush on our diving coach. This morning she practically drooled on his clipboard."

Brooke laughed.

"You'd drool, too," I told her. "He's totally dreamy."

"Dreamy is good," Brooke said, nodding. "But you know what I think is the most important thing in a serious relationship?"

"What?" Tess and I both asked.

"Trust. If you can't trust the person you love, then you don't have anything," she said.

"I'd trust Brad with my life," I declared.

"Me, too," Tess cracked. "He's a *life*guard!"

"Go ahead," I said. "Laugh. But at least *I* know when a guy is sending me signals."

"What's that supposed to mean?" Tess asked.

It means that Cody is crazy about you! I thought. *And you are totally clueless.* But I wasn't going to tell her. Not yet. It was more fun watching him try to get the message across.

"Figure it out," I said as I hopped out of the hairdresser's chair. "I'm going to get a facial."

After the salon and a few hours of shopping, we stopped at a café a few blocks from our house. It was a great place. It even had an outdoor roof garden overlooking the street.

Tess and I ordered sodas and bagels. Brooke went to make a phone call and change into a fancy dress for her date with Dad.

While we were waiting for Brooke, Tess leaned over the balcony railing to see what was happening on the street. "Emily! Look who's cruising down there on his skateboard!"

I ran to see. It was Ryan—the punk from the pool! He was skateboarding in our direction. I thought about how he made me look stupid in front of Brad. "It's payback time!" I grinned.

Tess nodded. "Yeah!"

We couldn't resist. The temptation was too great! Tess and I ran and grabbed a big pan of water from the waiter's station. Then we carried it over to the edge of the balcony.

"Hey, Ryan!" I called. "Come out of your pike—'cause here comes the water!" Then we dumped the whole pan of water on him! Ryan got totally soaked.

Tess and I slapped palms and doubled over, laughing. Ryan looked up and saw us laughing at him. For a minute, I thought he might come into the café and try to start something. But he just picked up his skateboard and walked on down the street.

Dripping wet!

Serves him right, I thought.

After our snack, we hurried home so that Brooke and Dad could go out on their date. When we got there, Nigel was in the living room, asleep in a chair.

"Wow, you women look nice," Dad said as we came in.

Tess and I twirled around to show off our new hairstyles. But Dad was looking only at Brooke. She wore a long black dress with lacy sleeves.

"Brooke's son should be here any minute," Dad said. "You three can hang out with Nigel tonight. Won't that be fun?"

"Oodles," I said flatly. But inside, I couldn't help wondering what Brooke's son would be like.

The doorbell rang.

"Oh, that must be him now," Brooke said.

Tess and I ran to the gate. We were about to meet the kid who might be our new brother—if everything worked out right.

I pulled open the gate and gasped.

It was Ryan!

CHAPTER TWELVE

"You?" I croaked. *"You're* Brooke's son?"

Ryan glared at me and Tess. "Can I come in?" he asked. He was still soaking wet.

Brooke came up behind us. "Oh, no! Ryan! What happened?" she cried, staring at him.

Uh-oh, I thought. *It's all over.*

But Ryan played it cool. "I wiped out on my skateboard," he said. "I fell into the pool."

"Well, let's get you upstairs and changed before you catch cold," Dad said. "I've got a bathrobe you can wear. We'll toss your clothes in the dryer. Come on—right this way."

Ryan followed Dad and Brooke. As soon as they were gone, Tess grabbed my arm. "I can't believe he didn't tell on us."

I shook my head. "Why did he cover for us?"

A few minutes later, they all came back downstairs. Ryan's clothes were dry.

Dad said good night and told us to have fun. "I'm counting on you to make Ryan feel right at home, okay?" he whispered to me and Tess.

We nodded.

"And if you have any problems," Dad added, "you can, uh, talk to Nigel."

We glanced at Nigel. He was still snoring away.

"Okay, Dad," I said. "We'll be fine. Go."

When they were gone, Tess and I turned to Ryan.

"How come you didn't tell on us?" Tess asked.

"Because I'm not a rat," he said.

"Spare us the Prison Code of Honor," Tess said, crossing her arms. "You didn't tell because now you've got one up on us. You can use it later when you really want revenge. Right?"

"You're not as dumb as you look," Ryan said.

Tess rolled her eyes. "So what was all that stuff about growing up in foster homes?"

Ryan didn't answer. He glanced at Nigel. "I thought this guy was your Dad's agent. What's he doing snoozing on your chair? Does he live here?"

"He thinks he does," Tess answered.

"Whatever," Ryan said. Then he turned to go. "Well, bye, kids. I'm out of here."

"You can't just leave," Tess said.

"Watch me," he said, and turned to leave.

"Why do you have to be so rude?" I asked him.

"I wouldn't expect you two to understand," he

said. "You're perfect little people with perfect lives."

"We're not perfect," Tess told him.

"Nobody is," I chimed in. "And our lives aren't perfect, either."

"Yeah, right," Ryan said. "Like everything you've ever tried hasn't worked out."

"I can't do a reverse dive," Tess said.

"That's just some stupid dive for some dumb competition," Ryan said. "Why does it matter so much to you?"

"My mother was a ballerina," Tess said softly. "Diving is as close as I'll ever get."

Ryan snorted. "That's so lame."

I put my hands on my hips. "You know, just because your dad got married again doesn't mean he won't love you anymore."

"Who asked you, Munchkin?" Ryan sneered.

"I'm Monster," I told him.

"*I'm* Munchkin," Tess said.

"Whatever," Ryan replied. "And by the way," he added, "I just decided to join the diving team."

My jaw dropped. How could he do this to me?

This was the guy who might end up as our brother?

"See you around, losers." He grabbed his skateboard and walked out of the house.

CHAPTER THIRTEEN

Tess and I woke Nigel up as soon as Ryan walked out. We tried to get him to help. But he was useless. The best he could do was call Dad on his cell phone, at the restaurant.

So Dad and Brooke raced home. They searched the whole neighborhood for Ryan, with no luck. Finally, near midnight, they came back empty-handed—and found him sitting on our steps.

Tess and I were asleep by then, so I don't know how Dad handled it. But knowing Dad, he was probably great.

He would be a terrific father for Ryan, I guess. But would Ryan be such a great brother? It didn't seem very likely.

Things didn't get much better the next day, at diving practice. Ryan did what he'd said he would. He joined the team!

I couldn't believe it. I knew he did it to get back at me.

"I'm sorry, Emily," Brad said. He tried to break

the news to me gently. "I know you've been working really hard on your dives. But you've got to agree that Ryan is a real plus for the Squids. And we want to win that meet, don't we?"

"Yes, Brad," I said. "Absolutely."

"I still want you around, though," Brad said.

I loved the sound of *those* words. "You do?" I gazed up into his bluer-than-blue eyes.

"Definitely," Brad said, nodding. "Hey, you're the alternate. If anyone can't dive, we'll put you in."

The alternate? I thought. *That's like being Miss Runner-Up. It's nothing.*

Brad gave me another one of his amazing smiles. "So can I count on you, Emily?" he asked.

"Always," I said, trying not to sound depressed.

The rest of the morning was pretty weird. Ryan was a really amazing diver. But he wouldn't speak to anyone on the team. So of course we didn't speak to him.

"You were looking good today," I told Tess as we walked home. "Your reverse pike is really coming along."

"Ryan's is better," she said.

As we came around the corner, we saw Nigel's car sitting in front of our house.

"Mr. Sleaze is back again," Tess said.

"What does he want this time?" I asked.

"Let's find out," Tess said with that gleam in her eye.

I knew exactly what she meant. The intercom!

We raced into the living room and punched the intercom button. Then we leaned close to the speaker, so we could hear.

There were two people talking—but it wasn't Nigel and Dad. It was Nigel and Brooke!

And when I heard what Brooke was saying, I nearly fell over. I couldn't believe my ears!

"Yes," Brooke said. "I would love to rent a house in Italy with Max. It would be great to spend time with him, alone."

Tess and I gasped. Brooke was talking about moving to Italy with Dad. *Without* us!

"But what about the children?" Nigel asked her. "You can't just leave them with some stranger."

"Why not?" Brooke said.

"No," Nigel insisted. "They're staying with me— that's it."

Tess and I stared at each other in horror.

"You'd take them for the whole summer?" Brooke asked.

"Of course," Nigel said. "What would *you* do? Send them off to some boarding school?"

"Great idea," Brooke said. "Send them away. It's not easy for Max and me to get to know each other with three kids running around."

Dad would never go along with this. No way. Even Nigel knew that. Because the next thing he said was, "Max won't go along with that."

"He'll have to come around in his own time," Brooke said. "By the way—how much is Max worth?"

I gasped again. I was so shocked I could hardly breathe.

"I can't believe this!" Tess whispered.

"Shhh," I said.

"If I didn't know better, I'd think you were just after his money," Nigel said.

"Okay, you caught me," Brooke answered. "I admit it."

"Ahhhh!" Tess cried.

That was enough. I slapped the Off button on the intercom.

"What are we going to do?" I moaned. "She's just after Dad's money!"

"Big-time," Tess said. "Boy, she really fooled me."

Neither of us knew what to do next. We went outside, to the courtyard. That was one of our favorite places to go and think.

"Emily, do you think we should tell Dad?" Tess whispered.

"Where is he, anyway?"

I shook my head. "Who knows? He's probably out shopping for an engagement ring! And it's all our fault. We're the ones who put up that billboard."

"Hey, Brooke didn't even answer our ad, remember?" Tess said. "Debbie did."

"Do you think she's still available?" I mumbled.

Tess didn't answer. She knew it was hopeless. Dad was already madly in love with Brooke. How were we supposed to tell him that the woman of his dreams was a fake?

He probably wouldn't believe us anyway.

Then Nigel burst into the courtyard. He was wearing his newest silk suit and alligator shoes. "Ducklets!" he said. "What's wrong? Why the long faces?"

"Don't try and act all cheery for us," Tess said. "We heard you talking to Brooke. Where did she go, anyway? Did she sneak out the back way so she wouldn't get caught?"

"Oh, dear," Nigel said. "I was hoping to spare you two the ugly truth. How much did you hear?"

"*Everything*," I answered. "They're moving to Europe and sending us to boarding school."

"And she's after his money," Tess added.

"Oh. Then you missed the part about her three ex-husbands?" Nigel asked.

Three ex-husbands? Oh, man. I put my head in my hands. "I thought Brooke loved Dad," I moaned.

"Well, kiddies," Nigel said, "it's time you learned that people aren't always what they appear to be."

I figured he was right. Look how wrong we were about Brooke. And about Nigel, too! Who would have thought he would offer to take care of Tess and me?

"You've got to help us, Nigel," I pleaded. "That woman's going to hurt Daddy. And he's been through enough already. We've got to stop her!"

A sneaky smile spread across Nigel's face. But this time I didn't mind. Nigel was on our side. And sneaky was just what we needed!

"I've got an idea for how we can get rid of her," Nigel said. "But it's a rather nasty plan. I'll need your help."

"Anything to save Dad," Tess said.

I nodded. "We'll do it," I told him. "Anything!"

CHAPTER FOURTEEN

"Hello, may I speak to Brooke?" I said into the phone the next afternoon. This was Step One in Nigel's big plan.

"Sure," a woman answered. "Is this one of Max's kids?"

"Yes, this is Emily," I said.

"Hi, Emily. This is Debbie. Remember me, from the museum? I work for Brooke, in her eyeglass shop."

"Oh, hi!" I said. *Debbie is nice,* I thought. *Too bad she didn't end up with Dad.*

Then I thought of something else. If Brooke was such a slime, how come Debbie was her best friend?

Brooke had *everyone* fooled!

"Gee," Debbie said. "Brooke was right here a minute ago. She must have just stepped out. Can I take a message?"

Tess was standing beside me, listening. "Tell her to come over here," Tess whispered.

I nodded. "Debbie, could you please tell her Dad needs to see her as soon as possible?" I said.

"Sure, honey," Debbie said. "I'll be sure to give her the message."

"Thanks," I said. Then I hung up.

"Step One—accomplished," Tess said.

"And Nigel's taking care of Step Two," I added.

"Let's go watch," Tess said.

We crept downstairs and peeked into Dad's studio. Nigel was just introducing Dad to a really gorgeous brunette named Fifi.

"Max," Nigel said. "Get out your drawing pad. Look what I brought you. Inspiration!"

Dad had a blowtorch in his hands. "No, thanks," he said. "I don't need a model today, Nigel. I'm working on my sculpture—just like you wanted."

"Oh, come on," Nigel begged. "Just do a little sketching as a favor for me. This poor young woman hasn't eaten in a week. She really needs the modeling work, okay?"

Dad sighed. "Well, I guess I could use some new ideas," he said. "But if I do this, Nigel, I don't want to hear another word from you about how I've been wasting time."

"No problem," Nigel said. "Where do you want her?"

"Well, how about on the sofa over there?" Dad said, pointing.

Fifi lay down on the couch. "Like this?" she asked.

"That's fine," Dad answered.

Nigel glanced over to where we were hiding and gave us the thumbs-up sign. Then he reached into a shopping bag he had brought along. He pulled out a bottle of wine and two glasses.

"What's that for?" Dad asked when he saw Nigel opening the bottle.

"I'm thirsty," Nigel said.

"Well, I'm working," Dad said. "I don't want anything to drink."

"Fine," Nigel answered. But he poured some wine into both of the glasses anyway.

"That is really low," I whispered to Tess. "It looks like Dad and that model are having a date."

"Exactly!" Tess said. "It's just what Brooke deserves!"

Nigel gave us one of his slimy smiles. Then he slipped out the back door.

About twenty minutes later, Brooke pushed the buzzer at the gate. But we didn't answer it. That was part of Nigel's plan, too. He wanted Brooke to walk in and catch Dad with Fifi.

A moment later Brooke let herself in through the side door. The timing was perfect—or awful, depending on how you looked at it.

Just as Brooke walked into the studio, Dad leaned over Fifi to adjust one of the couch pillows. When he bent down, Fifi reached up and kissed him.

Brooke saw the whole thing. You should have seen her face. It turned ash-white. And then her eyes filled up with tears.

She spun around and ran out the side door. She never saw Dad jerk back, startled, and ask Fifi, "Why did you do that?"

"Wow," Tess whispered. "I guess it worked."

"Did you see Brooke's face?" I said. "She looked so crushed. I feel sort of guilty."

Tess gulped, too. But she tried to sound tough. "She's a gold digger," she said firmly. "We had to do it."

"Well, if we did the right thing, then how come we feel so crummy?" I asked.

Tess couldn't answer that.

And I had a really bad feeling. Maybe we *didn't* do the right thing, I thought. Maybe we blew it!

CHAPTER FIFTEEN

Tess and I both felt awful for the next three days. Almost as awful as Dad. He was Mr. Miserable, moping around his studio. He kept calling Brooke, dozens of times each day. But she wouldn't speak to him.

I guess Tess and I should have been happy. But we weren't. We couldn't stand seeing Dad so sad again.

The only person who seemed tickled pink was Nigel. He hung around the house grinning like a cat. "Any word from the gold digger?" he asked as he waltzed in one morning.

"None," I answered. "She won't talk to Dad."

"Splendid!" Nigel beamed. "Don't say Uncle Nigel doesn't take care of things for you. Right?"

"Right," I mumbled, and dragged into my room.

I started to pack or the diving meet later that morning. "Is Dad coming to the meet?" I asked Tess.

She shook her head. "He said he has to work," she answered, stuffing a towel into her bag. "His new show opens in two days. He's busy."

Wow, I thought. Dad *never* skipped our meets!

All around, things were terrible. But when Tess and I got to the pool, I have to admit, I started to get excited. Diving meets are pretty cool. Lots of people show up just to watch, so it makes you want to do your best even more. And it's really fun hearing your name announced over the loudspeaker.

Of course, my name wasn't going to be announced today. Since Ryan had joined the team, I wouldn't be diving. I was just the alternate.

Oh, well. At least I didn't have to be nervous about my dives.

Cody's dad had brought the sound equipment. Cody was the announcer. He sat with the three judges at the judging table, which was set up on one side of the pool.

"Our first diver for Palos Verdes is Jenny Smith on the three-meter board," Cody said.

Jenny did a pretty good forward tuck with a half twist. All three judges gave her scores of six.

"They're off to a good start," I said nervously. I looked around at my team members. That's when I realized Ryan wasn't there. Where was he?

"Now diving for the Squids is Carol Clarke," Cody announced.

I couldn't watch. I kept scanning the crowd, trying to find Ryan. We needed him if we were going to win. How come he wasn't here yet?

"Has anyone seen Ryan?" I asked Kristen, who was sitting next to me.

"There he is now," she said.

I peered through the crowd. Ryan's bleached hair was easy to spot. He was making his way toward us. But he was fully dressed!

Tess was already on her way to the five-meter platform for her first dive. She glanced at me, alarmed. "Why doesn't he have his bathing suit on?"

Before I could answer, Brad came up and patted her on the back. "Tess, the reputation of our swim club rests on your shoulders," he said to her.

She gulped.

"So go out there, relax, and have fun," he added.

I watched my sister climb to the top of the high board. She took her time, which was good. Then she launched herself into the water.

"Great!" Kristen and Julianne cheered when Tess came up.

The judges thought her dive was pretty good, too. They gave her scores of six and seven.

Tess climbed out of the pool.

"Nice one," Ryan said.

Tess scowled at him. So did Brad.

"Why aren't you dressed?" Brad snapped. "You're late! Get your suit on!"

"I'm not diving today," Ryan said.

"What?" Brad yelled. "Don't play with me, kid. Of course you're diving!"

"I can't," Ryan said. He pointed to a bandage on his leg. "I just got a new tattoo. It has to stay out of the water forty-eight hours. Doctor's orders."

Brad practically exploded. "That's just great! I should have known I couldn't count on you! Now we're short a diver."

"No, you're not," Ryan said. He glanced at me. "You've got Emily."

Yikes! I hadn't been practicing that much lately. Not since I became an alternate.

Now the whole team was counting on me!

"Emily," Brad said, motioning me over to him. "I've been watching you. You've been looking really good lately."

"Thanks, Brad," I said. "So have you."

Brad didn't seem to hear me. "So come on, Emily," he said. "Give it all you've got."

Okay, I thought. *I can do this. Can't I?*

Well, I tried, anyway. I gave the team three good dives. They weren't spectacular, but most of them scored sixes. We were still in the running.

Tess did two more great dives. She was diving really well.

But so were the kids on the Palos Verdes team. When the last round came up, the teams were tied.

"Looks like you're the last diver, Emily," Brad said. "So it's all up to you."

My knees were shaking as I climbed to the three-meter board. I looked down at the water. *Why did Ryan do this to me?* I wondered.

Cody picked up the microphone and announced my name. "The winner of this meet will be decided by Emily Tyler's final dive," he said. "She needs a combined score of at least twenty-two to win for the Westside Squids."

Talk about pressure! My heart pounded as I stood there. But I tried to remember everything Brad had taught me. Legs together. Head down.

I made my approach, jumped, and dove.

Yes! I could tell as I hit the water—it was a good one!

When I came up, the crowd was clapping and cheering. I shook the water out of my eyes and glanced at the judges.

All three of them gave me eights! That was a great score—and it meant the Squids won!

Brad was waiting at the edge of the pool to help me out. "I knew you could do it," he said. "Way to go, Emily!"

Then he actually kissed me! Okay, it was only on the cheek—but he kissed me!

I floated through the next hour. The whole team celebrated at the pool. I ate two hot dogs with mustard and drank two sodas. Then I felt sick.

Finally, when everyone began to drift away, Tess and I went up to Ryan.

I looked him straight in the eye. "How come you lied to Brad so I could dive?" I asked.

"What makes you think I lied?" Ryan asked.

I reached down and ripped the bandage off his leg. "No tattoo," I said, pointing.

Ryan gave me an embarrassed smile. "Okay, you caught me," he admitted. Then he shrugged. "I wanted you to dive, Emily. I mean, you've worked hard for the team. I haven't."

"Wow," Tess said. "That's so...so nice!"

He looked down at the ground. "Yeah, well."

"So how is your mom?" Tess asked him quietly.

Ryan glanced up. "She'd be okay if your dad hadn't cheated on her," he answered, scowling.

I decided I had to set the record straight.

"He didn't," I said quickly. "Our dad isn't like

that. All she saw was some model Nigel brought over. It was all just a setup."

"A setup?" Ryan repeated. "What are you talking about?"

Tess put her hands on her hips. "Maybe your mom shouldn't have lied to our dad about her three ex-husbands."

"All she wanted was his money," I added.

Ryan looked at us like we were nuts. "What are you talking about? My dad's the only ex-husband she has. And her business is doing very well. She doesn't need your dad's money."

"But we overheard her, on the intercom—" I started to say. Then, all at once, I got it.

So did Tess.

"*Nigel!*" we both cried.

"He always wanted Dad and Brooke to break up," I said.

"He must have tricked us," Tess said.

Ryan snapped his fingers. "He came to see my mom one day at the store," he said. "He kept fiddling with something in his pocket. I'll bet it was a tape recorder."

"And then he edited the tape!" I guessed. "Maybe he made it sound like your mom said things she didn't really say. I've seen that on TV."

What a jerk! I couldn't believe even Nigel would do something that awful!

Then Ryan said, "I knew that Nigel guy was a slime, anyway. If anyone is stealing your dad's money, it's him."

"What do you mean?" I asked.

"I saw him," Ryan explained. "I was skateboarding in an alley one day. Nigel was at this warehouse, with some truck driver. They were loading up fake sculptures. Copies of your dad's stuff."

"No way," I whispered, shocked.

Ryan nodded. "Yes. Nigel was talking about how much money he was going to make on the side."

"I *knew* he was a sleaze!" Tess cried.

"And a crook," I added.

"We should warn your father," Ryan said.

I shook my head. "He'll never believe us," I said. "He trusts Nigel."

"He'll believe it if he hears it straight from Nigel," Tess said slowly.

"Yeah, like that's going to happen," Ryan scoffed.

"Maybe it will," Tess said, sounding excited. "Come on, I've got an idea. But we're going to need Cody's help!"

CHAPTER FIFTEEN

Tess wouldn't tell Ryan and me her idea. Not yet. She was in a hurry to find Cody. He had already left the pool.

We spotted him an hour later at the Venice boardwalk.

"Whoa!" Ryan said, staring at Cody in the distance. "What happened to him?"

Cody was sitting all by himself, playing a Gameboy. But that wasn't the weird part.

It was his spiked hair. And his earring. And his nose ring. And his leather jacket.

In one hour he had gone from normal to totally punked out.

"What's *that* all about?" I wondered.

"He looks like me," Ryan joked.

Tess shrugged. "Wait here. Let me talk to him." She walked up to him. Ryan and I crept closer so we could hear.

"Cody, what did you do to yourself?" Tess asked.

Cody sighed. "Okay, I know it sounds desperate," he said. "But I've tried everything to get your sister's attention. Concert tickets. T-shirts. Hanging around her all the time. And I've gotten nowhere. Right after the diving meet, she headed straight for that punk, Ryan! It's obvious your sister goes for bad boys—so here I am. If Tess doesn't get the message that I like her now, I'm just going to give up."

Oh, boy, I thought. *He thinks Tess is me!*

My sister didn't say anything for a moment.

"Emily, what's wrong?" Cody asked her.

"I'm *Tess*," she told him.

You should have seen Cody's face. Five shades of red. "Oh, man," he said finally. "I'm dead."

Tess grabbed his face and planted a kiss on his cheek. "No, you're not!" she said. "You're the best. I like you, too! But we can't talk about that right now. Cody, we need your help!"

He gazed into her eyes, looking all goofy. "Anything," he said. "Just name it."

Tess motioned for Ryan and me to join them. Then she told us all her plan. Basically, she wanted Cody to catch Nigel on tape—talking about how he was ripping off Dad. Then we'd play the tape for Dad—and he'd see the truth.

"We need the tape before the big gallery opening tomorrow night," Tess said. "I'll barf if we have to listen to another one of Nigel's speeches about how he made Dad into the famous artist he is today."

"But how are we going to get Nigel to talk about the copies and stuff?" I asked.

"Easy," Tess said. "We'll show Nigel the plans for Dad's new masterpiece."

Ryan nodded. "As bait?" he asked.

"Right," Tess said, nodding. "Nigel won't be able to wait. He'll take the plans to the rip-off artist today and copy them. We just have to follow him—and record the whole thing."

"Great," I said. "Let's go!"

Everything fell into place perfectly. The next morning, Nigel took the bait and ran with it—straight to his rip-off artist's warehouse.

"I need as many copies as you can make," Nigel told the guy. "I'm going to be rich! I'll make so much money selling Max Tyler knockoffs, I won't need him anymore!"

Cody hid behind a stack of boxes and caught the whole thing on tape. He met us back at the house a few hours later. "Here's the tape. I turned it into a rap," Cody said, grinning. "Wait till you hear it. It's a great mix!"

Whatever, I thought. Just as long as Dad knew it

was for real—and that Nigel had spoiled everything for him and Brooke.

"Come on," Tess said. "The gallery opening has already started."

Tess, Cody, and I hurried back to our house. Dad's studio was cleaned up, and his new sculptures were displayed.

The place was filled with people, all dressed up. They were looking at Dad's art. There was a big table with fancy food and drinks. Vases of flowers were everywhere.

But Dad was nowhere in sight.

"Where *is* he?" Nigel asked us. "Your father is the star. He should be here."

"I don't know," I said. "We'll go find him."

We hunted around and found Dad in a back office. He was leaving Brooke another message on her phone machine. "Please call me," he said. "I really want to talk to you. I miss you."

"Dad?" Tess said when he hung up. She held the tape out to him. "You've got to listen to this."

"Not now, girls," Dad said, sighing. "Later."

"But, Dad," Tess pleaded.

"Later," Dad repeated. Then he headed slowly toward the gallery. He looked totally miserable.

"How come Brooke isn't here?" I whispered to

Tess. "I thought Ryan was going to tell her the whole story."

Tess shrugged. "Maybe she didn't believe him."

"Dad won't believe us about Nigel, either," I said. "Unless he hears it for himself."

I grabbed the tape from Tess's hands.

"Emily, what are you doing?" she asked.

"Come on," I said. "Nigel is making his big speech right now. Let's do it!"

Tess and Cody followed me. We pushed our way through the crowd until we reached the front. Nigel was standing at a microphone, telling everyone how great *he* was. How *he* had discovered Dad. And made him into a star.

"Cody, where's your boom box?" I whispered.

Cody ran and got it. He set it on the floor near Nigel's microphone. Nigel was so busy talking, he didn't notice.

Tess and I rushed over. Tess grabbed the mike.

"Is anyone here buying this baloney?" she asked loudly.

Nigel looked shocked.

I leaned in to the mike. "You want to hear some straight talk?" I asked the crowd. "Listen to this. Crank it up, Cody!"

Cody hit the Play button and the tape started.

Dad marched toward the front of the room. "What are you doing?" he called angrily.

"Just listen, Dad," I begged.

The tape blasted through the sound system. It was a mix of funky music and Nigel's voice.

"I need as many copies of that as you can make—can make," Nigel said on the tape. "Can make—make—make. I'm going to be rich—rich—rich—filthy rich. Selling Max Tyler knockoffs—knockoffs—knock—knock—knockoffs!"

Dad's mouth dropped open. There was no doubt about it. That was definitely Nigel's voice.

"Nigel?" Dad said.

Nigel didn't answer at first. He just stood there, looking trapped.

"Tell Dad how you've been forging his sculptures," I said to Nigel.

"And selling fakes to all these honest people!" Tess added.

The crowd gasped. Dad got a funny look in his eyes, as if he was seeing Nigel clearly for the first time. "Nigel, is this true?" he demanded.

Nigel squirmed. He knew he'd been caught red-handed. "If you ask me, you should have sent those two nosy little brats to boarding school a long time ago!" he blurted out.

The crowd began to murmur.

Nigel slapped a hand to his mouth. "Oops. Did I say that out loud?"

"Yeah, Nigel, you did," Dad said, glaring at him. "You're fired. And lose the phony British accent. Everyone knows you're from New Jersey."

Nigel stormed out, with the whole room full of people staring at him.

It was obvious that Dad was in a really bad mood by now.

"Sorry, everyone," he said. "But the party's over. Please go home."

Everyone left quietly. Soon Dad, Tess, and I were the only ones left in the room.

Dad pulled us close to him. "Monster, Munchkin," he said. "From now on, it's going to be just the three of us. Our family. No outsiders."

"Not even me?" a voice asked.

We all turned around to see Ryan standing behind us.

"Ryan," Dad said. His face started to look hopeful. "Is your mom here?"

"No." Ryan shook his head. "But she asked me to come over here—and tell you to turn on the news."

"The news?" Dad asked. He sounded puzzled. Then he gave me and Tess a worried glance.

"Don't look at us!" I said quickly. "We have no idea what's going on!"

All of us ran to the television and turned it on. There was Kitty Buxbaum, the news reporter. She was standing on Sunset Boulevard—right in front of Dad's billboard!

"Well," Kitty reported, "It seems Billboard Dad is at it again. There's another message over the Sunset Strip—but this time, it's *for* him!"

The camera zoomed in on the billboard. The word TAKEN was painted across it in red letters!

"We don't know who the lucky lady is," Kitty went on. "But it just goes to show that it does pay to advertise!"

Dad whirled around. "I thought I told you kids never to do something like this again!" he said.

"We didn't do it!" Tess cried, holding up her hands.

"Honest!" I added.

"Then who did?" Dad asked.

Ryan grinned at Dad as if he had just won the lottery or something.

A moment later a car horn honked in front of the house.

Dad ran outside. Big surprise—Brooke was there, waiting for him!

Dad's smile was so big, I thought his face might split. "What's going on?" he asked Brooke.

Brooke shrugged. "I figure the billboard says it all."

"Well, not quite all," Dad said. Then he took her in his arms and kissed her.

"Yes!" Tess and I cheered, jumping up and down.

So everyone lived happily ever after. Tess and Ryan and I turned out to be great step-siblings. Cody was a happy guy, too, now that he and Tess were finally together.

The only person who didn't live happily ever after was Nigel. We saw him once, selling ugly dog paintings on the beach.

But of course, he deserved it.

So everything ended up perfectly, except for one thing.

Brad never did seem to figure out that I was the woman of his dreams. If only there was *some* way to get the message into his head!

But then I came up with the perfect answer.

The next time you're driving down Sunset Strip, keep your eyes peeled—for Billboard Twin!

IT'S YOUR FIRST CLASS TICKET TO ADVENTURE!

All New Feature Length Movie!

Own it only on Video!

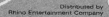

IT DOESN'T MATTER IF YOU LIVE AROUND THE CORNER...
OR AROUND THE WORLD...
IF YOU ARE A FAN OF MARY-KATE & ASHLEY OLSEN,
YOU SHOULD BE A MEMBER OF

MARY-KATE + ASHLEY'S FUN CLUB™

HERE'S WHAT YOU GET
OUR FUNZINE™
AN AUTOGRAPHED COLOR PHOTO
TWO BLACK & WHITE INDIVIDUAL PHOTOS
A FULL-SIZED COLOR POSTER
AN OFFICIAL FUN CLUB™ SCHOOL FOLDER
TWO SPECIAL FUN CLUB™ SURPRISES
FUN CLUB™ COLLECTIBLES CATALOG
PLUS A FUN CLUB™ BOX TO KEEP EVERYTHING IN.

TO JOIN MARY-KATE + ASHLEY'S FUN CLUB™,
FILL OUT THE FORM BELOW AND SEND IT, ALONG WITH
U.S. RESIDENTS $17.00
CANADIAN RESIDENTS $22.00 (US FUNDS ONLY)
INTERNATIONAL RESIDENTS $27.00 (US FUNDS ONLY)

MARY-KATE + ASHLEY'S FUN CLUB™
859 HOLLYWOOD WAY PMB 275
BURBANK, CA 91505

NAME:_____

ADDRESS:_____

CITY:_____ ST:_____ ZIP:_____

PHONE: (_____) _____

E-MAIL: _____

OR FAX YOUR CREDIT CARD ORDER TO US AT (818) 785-2275

CARD NUMBER:_____ EXP: _____

CARDHOLDERS NAME: _____

CARDHOLDERS SIGNATURE: _____

ATTN. CANADIAN AND INTERNATIONAL RESIDENTS
WE ARE NO LONGER ACCEPTING PERSONAL CHECKS DRAWN ON NON U.S. BANKS.
FOR EASE OF ORDERING, WE RECOMMEND PAYMENT VIA CREDIT CARD
(VISA OR MASTERCARD ONLY PLEASE)

CHECK US OUT ON THE WEB AT
WWW.MARYKATEANDASHLEY.COM